MEAN JAKE and the DEVILS

MEAN JAKE
and the DEVILS

by William H. Hooks

PICTURES BY DIRK ZIMMER

The Dial Press *New York*

Published by
The Dial Press
1 Dag Hammarskjold Plaza
New York, New York 10017

Designed by Jane Byers Bierhorst
First Printing

Library of Congress Cataloging in Publication Data
Hooks, William H. / Mean Jake and the devils.
Summary / Over the years Mean Jake has several run-ins
with Big Daddy Devil, Devil Junior, and Baby Deviline.
1. Children's stories, American.
[1. Devil — Fiction. 2. Short stories]
I. Zimmer, Dirk, ill. II. Title.
PZ7.H7664Me   [Fic]   81-65846
ISBN 0-8037-5563-5   AACR2   ISBN 0-8037-5564-3 (lib. bdg.)

For Billy and Lou

Contents

The Meanest Man in the World   *11*

Jake-o'-My-Lantern   *29*

Jake and the Fiddle   *43*

Author's Note   *63*

MEAN JAKE and the DEVILS

The Meanest Man in the World

"Look, GranAnna, look! There's the lights again. What is it?" whispered the boy.

"Old Jake's out there," answered the old woman. "Out there wandering through the swamp. Day and night, always wandering."

"It's the lights, I mean," explained the boy. "Is that what they call fox fire? Or is there somebody out there with a light, GranAnna?"

"Some folks calls it fox fire. But us that holds with the old ways knows

it's Jake. Always doomed to wander. On foggy nights like this you can see him plain and clear."

"Who's Jake, GranAnna?"

"I'll tell you how it come to be. But first we've got to say the magic words. Together, just the way I learned you."

GranAnna and the boy closed their eyes. The old woman snapped her fingers three times and they spoke together:

> Out of time and into grace
> We enter now a magic place.
> Protect us as we venture far
> And speak of things that never were
> But always are.

That Jake had a reputation when he was young. A reputation as the meanest man in the county.

Jake was a good-looking man and a clever one too. He was a tinker by trade; could fix anything made from metal, wood, or leather. And mean as he was to people, they kept bringing their broken shovels, their worn-out harnesses, and their leaky pots and pans for mending.

Jake was bound to pick a fight with any young man who dropped by. So after a while one of the families got wise and sent its pretty young daughter to have him mend a hole in a copper kettle.

The pretty young girl came up the hill to Jake's place, smiling.

"Morning, Mister Jake," she said.

"And a fair morning to you," said Jake, as nice as ever you please.

"Such a pleasant man," thought the girl. "And a good-looking one at that. I don't know what my brothers were talking about. They must be jealous."

So the pretty young girl showed Jake the hole in the kettle that need-ed mending.

"Only take a minute," said Jake. "And you'll have a kettle good as new."

The girl stood around watching Jake. Jake smiled at her and made a little joke. And soon he had her giggling and having herself a good time.

When he just about had the kettle fixed, he said, "Why don't you rest a minute on my three-legged stool? You've got a long walk back home."

The girl thanked Jake and sat down very ladylike on the stool. It

wobbled a little bit under her, and she thought it must be sitting on a bumpy spot on the ground. She wiggled to settle the stool. And *bang!* A leg popped off, and the poor girl rolled backwards into a mud hole where a fat pig was wallowing.

Jake laughed so hard, he got a stitch in his side.

When the girl scrambled up out of the mud hole, she saw that the stool had one leg sawed through. She was so mad Jake had tricked her that she grabbed the stool and flung it at him. He caught it with one hand and danced a jig while the girl tried to scrape mud off her dress.

"You're the meanest man in the county!" she shouted.

"Thank you," cried Jake, still dancing with the stool in his hand.

So the girl went on home with a kettle good as new and a fine dress just about ruined.

Jake couldn't have been more pleased. Now he had a reputation for being just as mean to women as he was to men.

Now, things work around in the strangest of ways. And every place has got its special season. Ours happens to be the fall, when fields are white with cotton and fox grapes cluster ripe and juicy on the vines. That's when Saint Peter chooses to walk this way.

Saint Peter had picked his day that year—a cool, sunny fall day. And who do you think was the first person Saint Peter bumped into? Mean Jake.

"Jake," said Saint Peter, "I don't know how deserving you are, but you're going to get three wishes today."

"You're not joking with me?" asked Jake.

"No, the rule says the first person I meet gets three wishes. I've got to stick by the rules. Name your first wish, Jake."

Jake looked at the three-legged stool he had used to trick the pretty girl. "I wish that stool would start to hopping up and down when anybody sits on it. And they can't get off until I tell the stool to halt."

Saint Peter's eyes walled back a little when he heard Jake's wish. But he was a man of his word.

"So granted," said Saint Peter. "Now, think careful, Jake, and don't go wasting your other wishes."

Jake didn't think but a second. He held out the hammer in his hand and said, "This is my wish number two: Anybody who picks up my hammer can't stop hammering until I tell the hammer to halt."

Saint Peter closed his eyes and made a face.

"Those are mean wishes, Jake. If I weren't a stickler for rules, I'd stop right here. But you've got one more wish coming."

Saint Peter hardly had the words out before Jake pointed to a bramblebush.

"See that bramblebush, Saint Peter?" cried Jake. "I wish that anyone who touches that bramblebush will get caught up in it and shook up in its brambly branches until I yell halt to it."

Saint Peter breathed a little prayer and said, "Your wish is granted."

Just before he left, Saint Peter said, "Be careful how you use those wishes, Jake."

He walked off into the clear autumn afternoon and vanished.

Word about Jake's meanness spread all over the country. Tough young men came from far and near to see if what people were saying about Jake was true.

The ones that got tricked into sitting on the stool went away hopping like frogs.

Those that tried Jake's hammer had stiff, sore arms for a week after Jake yelled "Halt!"

And the ones that managed to get around the hammer and the stool ended up caught in the bramblebush. Those poor boys staggered back home looking like they had been used for pincushions.

Soon Jake had the reputation for being the meanest man in the world.

He smiled and said, "Thank you, Saint Peter."

And poor Saint Peter was sorry he had been so strict about the rules.

Finally word reached all the way down to hell that Jake was the meanest person alive—and a lot of folks were claiming he was even meaner than the devil himself.

Now, that didn't sit too well with old Mister Big Daddy Devil. And it didn't sit too well with D.J.—that's what they called Devil Junior— who wanted to be just like Big Daddy Devil. Even little pudgy Deviline, the baby girl devil, was upset about it.

"It's probably just another rumor coming from up there," said Big Daddy Devil, trying to sound like he didn't put much stock in that kind of thing.

"It burns me up, Big Daddy," shouted D.J. "That Jake's trying to steal your reputation."

"It scorches me too, Big Daddy," cried Deviline. "Nobody can be as mean as my sweet Daddy Devil. I'd like to go upstairs and fix that Jake."

"Well," said Big Daddy Devil, "since this seems like a job for a child, why don't you handle it, Baby Deviline?"

So Baby Deviline grabbed her little pitchfork and hopped right upstairs.

When Jake saw her coming, he could tell she was a mean little devil. But she was a baby, so he wasn't worried.

"What do you mean trying to steal my daddy's reputation?" screamed little Deviline, shaking her pitchfork at Jake.

"Now, I can see you're a smart little devil," said Jake. "Why don't we sit for a minute and straighten this thing out?"

Jake pulled up a chair for himself and pointed to the stool for Deviline.

"That's more like it," said Deviline as she flicked her short stubby tail to one side and sat down.

Well, that stool started hopping, and poor Baby Deviline couldn't get loose. She screamed and hollered till her eyes were crossed, but Jake just laughed and let her bounce.

After a good long while, when Jake was worn out with laughing, he said, "Promise you'll never come bothering me again, and I'll let you go."

Deviline was out of breath, but she stammered, "I promise."

Jake shouted "Halt!" and the chair stopped.

Deviline hopped downstairs as fast as she could and told Big Daddy Devil and D.J. what had happened.

D.J. was mad as firecrackers.

"I'm going right up, Daddy, and fix that Jake. He can trick a baby but he can't hold a fire to a Devil Junior."

So he went upstairs.

"Have a seat," said Jake with a big smile.

"I'm on to your tricks," said D.J. "You're not going to trap me that way."

"Well, how about a game of catch?" cried Jake. With that he threw the hammer at D.J.

D.J. had to catch it or get bashed in the head. The second that hammer landed in D.J.'s big webbed hand, he started hammering.

He hammered all day and right into the night. He pleaded with Jake to set him free, but Jake just laughed.

At last Jake got sleepy and said, "Promise you'll never come messing around with me, and I'll let you go."

D.J. said, "I pr-pr-pr-pr-romise. Promise! Promise!"

"Halt!" shouted Jake. The hammer dropped from D.J.'s hands, and he staggered on downstairs.

"That Jake's the meanest thing I've ever seen," cried D.J.

That really upset old Big Daddy Devil. "Meaner than me?" he asked.

"I'm afraid so, Daddy," said D.J.

"Well, I see this is a man's job," said Big Daddy.

And he went on upstairs right in the middle of the night and rapped on Jake's window.

Jake didn't like to have folks disturbing his sleep, so he was pretty mad when he looked out the window. There was old Daddy Devil just as mad as Jake.

"I dee-double-dog-dare you to step out here in the yard!" shouted Big Daddy Devil.

Jake came right out of the house, still in his underwear.

"I don't take no dee-double-dog-dares from nobody!" cried Jake.

Big Daddy Devil swung his forked tail at Jake, but Jake hopped over

the swinging tail like it was a jump rope. Then he grabbed Big Daddy
Devil by the tail and slung him into the bramblebush.

Now, Big Daddy Devil had a tough skin, but this was no ordinary
bramblebush. It shook him and scratched him till he hollered for mercy.

"Who's the meanest person in the world?" asked Jake.

"You are!" cried Big Daddy Devil.

"Promise you'll never come messing around with me again, and I'll let you go," said Jake.

Big Daddy was quick with the promising.

"Halt, bramblebush!" shouted Jake.

Big Daddy Devil rose from the bramblebush and limped downstairs.

They say it took a week for Baby Deviline and D.J. to pick out all the bramble nettles that were stuck in Big Daddy's tough hide.

Mean old Jake lived to be nearly a hundred, they say. Stayed mean the whole time. But mean as he was, he couldn't trick the old Reaper forever. So he died, and the stool and the hammer and the bramblebush lost their powers.

Saint Peter sighed a big sigh of relief. "That's the last I'll be bothered with Jake," he said.

But he no more than had the words out of his mouth when there was Jake knocking at the pearly gates.

"Saint Peter, it's me!" cried Jake. "How about letting me in?"

"You abused your wishes," said Saint Peter. "You can't come in here."

With that, two angels pulled a cloud down behind the gates, and Saint Peter was gone.

Jake was old and tired, and he needed a place to rest. But he started down the road again. Pretty soon he came to the gates of hell. He was worn-out. He knocked and waited.

Baby Deviline was playing catch with a ball of fire not far from the gates. She heard the knock and ran to see who was calling.

The minute she saw Jake, she screamed, "Big Daddy! Help! Big Daddy! D.J.! He's here!"

Big Daddy and D.J. came running, and they all piled up behind the gates and stood there with their forked tails waving.

"Let me in," said Jake in a weak and weary voice.

"Put the extra bolt on the gate, D.J.," said Big Daddy.

"Please, I need a spot to rest," pleaded Jake.

"Go away!" screamed Deviline. "We promised never to mess around with you. And devils keep their promises."

"Where can I go?" asked Jake.

"Anywhere but here," said Big Daddy Devil.

"But it's dark," said Jake. "I need a light to find my way."

"Here," said Big Daddy Devil, handing Jake a ball of fire. "Go find a hell of your own."

"What did Jake do then?" asked the boy.

GranAnna took a deep breath and pointed toward the swamp.

"Jake took the ball of fire in his hands and he went wandering. He finally ended up in the Great Dismal Swamp, doomed by the devils to wander there forever. Look, child," said GranAnna, "he's moving behind the cypress tree right now."

Jake-o'-My-Lantern

"Now, watch careful, child. Look how I carve this pumpkin."

The boy stared as GranAnna's knife swiftly cut out a face.

"It's like a regular jack-o'-lantern," said the boy.

"But this is a Jake-o'-my-lantern," said GranAnna in a hushed voice. "And where the nose ought to be I carve a cross."

"Why, GranAnna? Does a Jake-o'-my-lantern have anything to do with mean old Jake?"

GranAnna looked around, then nodded her head.

"It does. This very night being Halloween, old Jake's going to leave the swamp."

"How? I thought he was doomed to wander there forever."

"Shh, shh," cautioned GranAnna. "It's getting dark. All sorts of evil spirits might be hovering around this night."

"Old Jake too?" asked the boy.

"Yes, yes," whispered GranAnna, hurrying the boy into the house. "Get inside and I'll tell you how it happened."

Jake had wandered well nigh a hundred years, carrying his ball of fire through the swamp. Always the same, day after day, night after night, and year after year. And I reckon it would have gone on like that forever if it hadn't been for Baby Deviline.

Now, you may wonder how Baby Deviline stayed a baby devil all that time. Well, devils don't change. They come the way they are. Either they come full-grown devils like Big Daddy Devil, or middle-sized devils like D.J., or little devils like Baby Deviline. And that's the way they stay.

Every year Big Daddy Devil would come upstairs and scout around for a week or more before Halloween. He was always on the lookout to do some mischief or work an evil deal with someone.

"D.J., I'm leaving you in charge down here," said Big Daddy Devil. "Think you can manage to tend all these fires and keep my pokers red-hot?"

"You can count on me, Big Daddy," boasted D.J.

And with that Big Daddy Devil went on upstairs and left D.J. in charge.

Baby Deviline was taking her nap when Big Daddy left, so she didn't get to say good-bye to him. Baby Deviline was apt to be out of sorts when she woke from her naps. Big Daddy always played a game of jacks with her after naptime.

"Where's my daddy?" cried Baby Deviline when she woke up. "I want my daddy."

D.J. was busy turning a bunch of hot iron pokers. "Hush that fuss!" he shouted.

"Where's Big Daddy?" asked Baby Deviline.

"Big Daddy's gone on upstairs. And I'm the boss now. So stop that whining and put some coals on the fire over there."

"I'm hungry," cried Deviline.

"No work, no food," said D.J. "Not one burned hoecake are you going to get until you help me stoke all of these fires."

Baby Deviline cried and dragged her feet and swished her little pointed tail. But D.J. was good as his word. He didn't let her have a mouthful until she helped stoke all the fires.

About the third day D.J. was restless and wondering what kind of good times Big Daddy must be having upstairs.

"Baby Deviline," he said to her, "you've turned out to be a right smart little firebug. I do believe you could tend this place as good as me."

"Nothing to it," said Baby Deviline.

"Then I'm going to let you be the boss while I step upstairs for a spell."

And before Baby Deviline could answer, D.J. was off in a puff of steam.

Baby Deviline said to herself, "Well, if I'm the boss, I'll just get my jacks out and catch up on my playing."

So Baby Deviline played jacks and ate burned hoecake and took long naps. And not once did she turn a poker or stoke a fire. Soon it grew so cold, she decided she would hop upstairs to get warm in the sunlight.

Baby Deviline was just beginning to thaw out when along came Big Daddy Devil.

"Hi, Daddy," she called. "I'm so glad to see you."

Big Daddy Devil smelled something wrong right away.

"Where's D.J.?" he roared.

"D.J.'s been gone a couple of days," answered Baby Deviline.

"Gone!" shouted Big Daddy. "Who's tending the fires?"

Baby Deviline shrugged her shoulders.

"You stay right here, Baby Deviline," said Big Daddy. "I'll find Mr. D.J. and be right back."

There was a big puff of smoke and Big Daddy Devil was gone.

"I sure wish Daddy would show me how to do that," said Baby Deviline.

In no time Big Daddy was back with a shamefaced D.J.

"Come on," ordered Big Daddy Devil. "Let's get on home."

They hopped right quick downstairs. Big Daddy couldn't believe his eyes. Every fire was dead. All his red-hot pokers were cold and gray.

"I'm finished!" wailed Big Daddy Devil. "Finished."

Big Daddy sat down and cried great hot salty tears. D.J. slunk around with his forked tail between his legs.

But Baby Deviline was thinking.

"Daddy!" she screamed. "Daddy, I've got it!"

Big Daddy kept on dropping hot salty tears in the dead ashes.

"Listen, Daddy," cried Baby Deviline. "I know where we can get some of our special fire to start over again."

Big Daddy Devil looked up. "Just ordinary fire won't work, Baby. We need a high-powered fire. We're done for."

"Listen, Big Daddy. You gave old Jake one of our fireballs, remember? He's still got it."

Big Daddy Devil brushed the hot salty tears from his eyes. He smiled and patted Baby Deviline on her cold little shoulder.

"Old Jake," he said. "Now, that's a man I can deal with."

So it happened on a night just like this. A night that set in with pink and purple skies. Pink for fair weather when the new day dawned, and purple for a sharp, crisp frost to ripen fox grapes and dust pumpkins with a silver coating.

It was the night before Halloween when Big Daddy Devil went up-stairs and headed for the Great Dismal Swamp, where old Jake was a-wandering.

Big Daddy Devil saw the light moving in the cypress trees. In an in-stant he was walking beside old Jake.

"Nice light you have there," he said to old Jake.

Old Jake was so tired of wandering, he didn't say a word. They walked on for a while. Big Daddy sure wanted to just grab the fireball, but devils can't take back gifts.

"I'd make you a good deal for some of that fireball," said Big Daddy.

"What kind of deal?" asked Jake.

"Oh, I was thinking you must be tired of wandering here in this swamp. I was thinking you must need a night off. I could arrange that for you."

Old Jake had been wandering the swamp for near a hundred years now. A night off sounded mighty sweet to him.

"You mean just one night off, or a night off every year?" asked old Jake.

"Well, I really couldn't promise more than one night."

"When will it be?" asked old Jake.

"What about Halloween night? But you could start right now," said Big Daddy.

"It's a deal," agreed old Jake.

And with that, Big Daddy Devil spit in the air, made a sign, and said a magic word. Then he turned old Jake away from the swamp, and they walked out.

"My, my," said old Jake. "It sure feels good to be walking on dry land."

The moment old Jake's feet dried out, he started thinking how he could outwit Big Daddy Devil and get himself a night off every year.

"Now I've kept my part of the bargain, let's break the fireball in half," said Big Daddy.

They were standing under a persimmon tree. Old Jake looked up and saw big, ripe, juicy persimmons hanging in the tree.

"I'm powerful hungry," said old Jake. "In fact I'm so hungry, I don't have the strength to break this fireball."

"Well, we can fix that right away," said Big Daddy. And he scrambled up the tree and started picking the juicy persimmons.

Quick as a rabbit, old Jake slipped his knife out of his pocket and cut a cross on the trunk of the tree.

Big Daddy was feeling good, thinking he would soon have half a fireball to kindle all his fires. He started down the tree with the juicy persimmons for old Jake.

Suddenly he saw the cross cut into the tree trunk.

"Traitor!" he screamed, throwing the persimmons at old Jake. "You're a cheat! You know my secret. It's not fair! You know the only thing that can stop me is a cross. You're not playing fair!"

Old Jake laughed and laughed. And he sat under the persimmon tree, eating the sweet juicy fruits all night long.

Now, old Jake had become as wise as he was old. Wandering in the swamp all those years, he had learned a lot. And he knew that come sun-up the devil would be freed from the spell.

Just before dawn he called out to Big Daddy Devil, "I've broken my

fireball in half. Give me a night off every year and I'll leave you half the fireball in a pumpkin under this persimmon tree."

Big Daddy Devil rumbled and rankled and shot off a lot of smoke, but he wouldn't agree to the deal.

The night sky began to fade. Time was running out for old Jake. He stood up and pretended he was leaving with the whole fireball.

"Hold on there!" roared Big Daddy Devil. "Maybe we can make a deal."

"Then I get one night a year when I can leave the swamp and walk on dry land. Agreed?"

"Agreed!" shouted Big Daddy Devil.

And just before the first sunbeam shot across the land, old Jake took his half of the fireball and ran back into the swamp.

Big Daddy Devil was stuck in the persimmon tree until the sun struck the trunk of the tree where old Jake had carved the cross. Then the spell broke and he jumped to the ground, grabbed the pumpkin with the ball of fire, and hurried downstairs.

Baby Deviline and D.J. were huddled in the cold ashes. Their teeth were chattering and their forked tails were covered with goose pimples.

"Quick!" cried Big Daddy Devil. "Light the fires with this fireball!"

Back in the swamp, old Jake rested on a soft bed of moss. He was mighty pleased to have outwitted Big Daddy Devil.

"I reckon I'll sleep all day," he said to himself. "I've got a big night ahead of me . . . it being Halloween."

The boy looked fearfully out into the night.

"Is old Jake outside?" he asked.

"Could be," answered GranAnna.

Then the old woman smiled and pointed to the glowing pumpkin in the window.

"Don't fret, child. The same sign that stops Big Daddy Devil stops old Jake too. That's why I made the nose on the pumpkin like a cross. True, on Halloween old Jake comes out of the swamp. But he'll never stop at a house with a Jake-o'-my-lantern."

Jake and the Fiddle

"Want me to play you a fiddle tune, GranAnna?" called the boy.

"Wait, child. You don't realize what you're saying." GranAnna quickly made a sign in the air with her left hand.

"Are you angry with me?" asked the boy.

"No, not angry," replied the old woman. "I'm scared for you."

"What do you mean?"

"Old Jake was the best fiddle player ever known in these parts. I'd hate to see you follow in his footsteps."

"I didn't know mean old Jake had a fiddle. How'd he get one out there in the swamp?"

"Put that fiddle back in the case and I'll tell you," said the old woman.

Long ago, folks still remembered that it was the devil who invented the fiddle. Devils were the only ones who had fiddles back then. Big Daddy Devil could put a spell on anybody with his fiddle playing. There was some that claimed D.J. was even better at fiddling than Big Daddy. But Baby Deviline took the cake. That little devil was a natural-born fiddler.

Folks around here used to gather for square dancing on the big holidays. Banjo pickers, guitar strummers, and mandolin players would come from as far off as Black Mountain. If any fiddlers turned up, the old folks would chase them away. They knew fiddle music could drive young people crazy.

Well, there was this big square dance one night on Halloween. The young folks were in a high fever of excitement. And the old folks were jumpy nervous. But come time for the dance to begin and not a fiddler turned up. The old folks settled back in their chairs while the young ones glided around the floor to the sweet, safe sounds of banjos and guitars.

Ordinarily the old folks would keep a sharp eye on the dancers. But

with no fiddle players around, they got careless. That's when it always happens. Never fails. At first the old folks didn't notice anything. But a feeling started creeping over them, sneaking up on them before they even knew it.

One crippled old lady turned and looked toward the dancers. She rubbed her eyes and cried, "The young folks! Look!"

All the old folks stared at the swirling couples flying around the room.

The crippled old lady cried again, "Fiddlers! There's fiddlers over there!"

Sitting in with the musicians were three fiddlers. Three fiddlers dressed in black with bloodred capes.

Try as they would, the old folks couldn't make a move. Their feet were rooted to the floor. So they just stood there and watched while the music went faster and faster. And the dance got wilder and wilder.

Finally the set came to an end. The young folks stopped dancing. The old folks could move again.

"Where you folks from?" one of the young men asked the fiddle players.

"We're a fiddling family from up Black Mountain way," answered the biggest fiddle player.

The old folks, being naturally more cautious, held back. So the big fiddle player stepped forward and offered his hand.

"I'm Big Daddy Duval," he said, real friendly like.

"And this here is my son, Duval Junior, and my daughter, Baby Duvaline."

Those fiddlers were such charmers, they had everybody offering them sarsaparilla and stuffing them with tea cakes in no time. The old folks never realized they were under a spell.

Came time for the next set of dances and the old folks edged their chairs close to the dance floor and started tapping their feet. The dancers broke into a grand right and left.

Then that Duval family really showed their colors. They flipped back their bloodred capes and cut loose on those fiddles. And not one of those poor country folks was smart enough to see them for the devils they were.

First, Big Daddy Devil took the lead. How he made that fiddle sing! Oh, it was a sweet sound like a bunch of nightingales singing their hearts out. The dancers swayed, and the young girls leaned close to the young men.

Then Big Daddy Devil played his fiddle wild and fast and the young folks raced around the floor. The girls' hair streamed out behind them

like the manes of wild horses on the run. Their hearts were pounding like they would burst, but Big Daddy went faster and faster. The dancers were just a blur.

At last Big Daddy played a final chord and bowed to D.J.

The dancers thought they would drop but D.J. never let them rest for a moment. He made his fiddle moan and cry; he made it sob and wail. And everybody in the room was moaning and wailing along with the music he played.

"Stop the music!" pleaded the young girls.

But the devils played on, and the dancers couldn't stop their feet. The old folks swayed in their chairs, caught in a trance.

Much as he hated to do it, D.J. finally had to give Baby Deviline her chance to shine.

Well, those poor folks didn't know what they had in store. Baby Deviline spit on her bow and set it to the fiddle. Her fiddle bow looked like a lightning bolt striking the strings. That little devil played mean, low-down reels and wild stomps and music meant to set your blood on fire. And she played it with such hurricane speed, the dancers flew around the floor.

They begged and pleaded and finally had no breath left to even plead. But their feet wouldn't stop moving. Young girls fainted and their partners kept dragging them around the floor in time to the music. Baby Deviline had them all in her spell.

"Now grab your partner and promenade home!" called Big Daddy.

Baby Deviline, still playing her fiddle at double-time speed, started leading the folks toward the door. They were following her two by two. She was headed straight for the fiery dungeons down below. And none of the dancers had the power to stop their feet.

Just as the procession was about to leave the room, the door flew open.

Baby Deviline was blinded by a powerful light that flashed in the dark doorway.

A hand reached in and snatched her fiddle.

"It's him!" she screamed.

Mean old Jake stood in the doorway with his glowing fireball in one hand and her fiddle in the other. He laughed and said, "You forgot. I get to come back on Halloween night every year. I've been wanting some fiddle music for the longest time to keep me company out in the swamp."

Old Jake's sudden appearance broke the spell the devils had on the people. Everybody scattered.

Big Daddy, D.J., and Baby Deviline disappeared in a puff of smoke. Old Jake vanished back into the swamp, carrying his fireball and the fiddle. And all the country folks hurried home, locked their doors, and pulled down the window shades.

Down below, Baby Deviline was throwing a fit.

"I want my fiddle!" she screamed.

"Here, Baby," said Big Daddy. "You can play my big fiddle."

"No!" screamed Baby Deviline. "If I don't get my fiddle back, I'm going to be sick and throw up on the red-hot pokers."

Then she rolled on the floor and squalled and beat her forked tail

around in the ashes till D. J. and Big Daddy were choking with the dust she raised.

"All right!" cried Big Daddy. "All right. I'll pop on upstairs."

In a flash Big Daddy was out in the swamp, walking beside old Jake.

"That was a pretty low trick you pulled back there at the dance," said Big Daddy Devil.

"Look who's talking," said Jake.

"Yes," said Big Daddy, "I can't think of anything lower than taking a child's plaything."

"Ha!" laughed old Jake. "That little devil is no ordinary child. And this here fiddle is no plaything."

"Why don't you give it back to her?" asked Big Daddy. "You can't even play it."

"I've got plenty of time to learn," said old Jake. "And when I learn it, I'm going to be better than any of you devils."

"Who's going to teach you how to play?" asked Big Daddy.

"You are," answered Jake.

That got Big Daddy so steamed up, smoke started escaping from his ears. It was bad enough to lose a fiddle. To give away the devils' secret of how to play one—that was too much.

Old Jake said, "Now that I've had a taste of leaving the swamp, I find it to my liking. I was thinking how nice it would be to pop out of the swamp every so often and do some fiddling at square dances—drive the dancers crazy."

"Now, hold on," cried Big Daddy. "Fiddle playing is for devils only. I've already stretched the rules by giving you Halloween night off every year."

"Well," said old Jake, "I guess I'll just have to keep this fiddle and learn to play it the best I can right here in the swamp."

Old Jake set the bow to the fiddle strings and started sawing away. The

scratchy noise sounded more like caterwauling than music. The terrible sound made Big Daddy's tough hide crawl.

It was getting near morning, and Big Daddy wanted to get down below before the sunlight caught him. And Jake's fiddling was getting on his nerves.

Old Jake noticed Big Daddy twitching, so he scraped the bow across the strings faster and faster.

Big Daddy gave a loud grunt and flew off in a puff of steam.

"Now I know just how to handle those devils!" cried old Jake.

Big Daddy was dog tired, but he went right to work on a new fiddle.

"Come on, D.J.," he called. "I need you to help me make Baby Deviline a new fiddle."

Big Daddy and D.J. worked all day making the fiddle. Baby Deviline slept fitfully the whole time. She squirmed and gnashed her teeth and flicked her tail about like she was having a nightmare.

Finally the fiddle was finished.

"You got my fiddle back!" yelled Baby Deviline, awake at last.

Big Daddy and D.J. winked at each other. Baby Deviline smiled and cuddled the fiddle close and went back to sleep.

In no time Big Daddy and D.J. were sound asleep and snoring deep.

Baby Deviline was the first to wake up. "What's that awful noise?" she cried

But D.J. and Big Daddy kept right on snoring.

She punched them with her little pitchfork. "Daddy! D.J.! Wake up!"

The big sleepy devils sat up and rubbed their eyes.

"What is it?" asked D.J. "It gives me the shivers up my back."

"Never heard such a horrible noise in my life," said Baby Deviline.

Big Daddy knew it was old Jake scraping away at the strings of the fiddle. But he didn't want to tell Baby Deviline that.

"Sounds like cats fighting to me," said Big Daddy. "They'll stop in a minute."

Big Daddy was wrong. The terrible scratchy noise went on all day.

The devils stuffed moss in their ears, but the screechy sound wormed its way right in.

Finally night came on. The devils were all frazzled out. Big Daddy dreaded the thought of trying to sleep with old Jake's screechy, scratchy fiddling.

Then suddenly it stopped.

The exhausted devils dropped right where they were and fell asleep.

Just as they were easing into deep peaceful slumber, old Jake cut loose on the fiddle again.

The devils woke with grunts and roars.

The terrible sound was ringing in their heads. In the night it seemed closer and louder.

"I can't stand it!" shouted D.J.

"I'm breaking out in a rash!" cried Baby Deviline.

By morning the devils were exhausted, but old Jake still sawed away on the fiddle.

"It's a contest of wills," mumbled Big Daddy to himself. "I'll show that Jake who can hold out the longest."

By the end of the third day the devils were convinced the awful sound would never stop. Big Daddy knew he had to deal with old Jake.

Baby Deviline and D.J. were in such a daze, they didn't even see Big Daddy leave. He popped upstairs and fell in beside old Jake.

"You're getting worse instead of better on that fiddle," said Big Daddy.

"Sounded pretty bad to me, too, at first," said Jake. "But now that I'm getting used to it, I kind of like it."

Old Jake raked the bow across the fiddle strings, making long screechy sounds. He danced around Big Daddy like a wild man.

Big Daddy gritted his teeth and poked his fingers in his ears.

Jake laughed and sawed away.

"Stop! Stop!" yelled Big Daddy.

But Jake scratched louder and louder with the fiddle bow.

"Stop," pleaded Big Daddy.

Jake sawed faster and louder.

"If you'll just stop, I'll tell you the magic words that will make you fiddle like a devil," cried Big Daddy.

Jake lifted the bow from the strings, and the terrible screeching stopped.

Big Daddy leaned over and whispered the magic words in Jake's ear.

Then the poor old devil tried to fly off in a puff of smoke. But he was too weak to make any steam, so he just staggered on downstairs.

Jake said the magic words and lifted the fiddle under his chin. He drew the bow across the strings. Sweet fiddle tunes floated over the land, riding the night mists out of the swamp. The devils slept soundly.

But they say a young girl woke up and heard the music that very first night. She wandered out into the swamp, following after the sound of it, and was never seen again.

"Is that the end of the story, GranAnna?" asked the boy.

"No. I reckon this story has no end."

"What do you mean?"

"After that, old Jake started popping up all over the place with his fiddle. He took a pure evil delight in setting young men on fire with his music. Pretty soon lots of young fellows started making fiddles of their own."

"I'll bet old Jake was jealous," said the boy.

"Not a bit. Jake liked nothing better than slipping up on them and whispering the magic fiddle words."

"What happened?"

"Them that used the words went wild and played music just like those devils did in olden times."

"But why were you afraid for me, GranAnna? Do old Jake and the devils still come to dances?"

"Well, not in the flesh like they used to. But, child, remember this. When you play that fiddle, just you be on guard for any whispering in your ear."

The old woman snapped her fingers three times. Then she and the boy whispered together:

> Protect us as we venture far
> And speak of things that never were
> But always are.

Author's Note

The stories in this book are based on tales I heard as a child growing up in the tidewater country of North Carolina. My two favorite storytellers were my grandmother and a great aunt. So in *Mean Jake and the Devils* I have combined them into a single person and named her Grananna.

"Jack tales" are common throughout the South. Sometimes Jack—or Jake as he was called—was a prankster, playing tricks for fun. But the mean old Jake that I heard about from my childhood storytellers was the character who most fascinated me. And because of this, perhaps to humor me, they built a great many stories around him. Later I became aware that rearranging events and shaping stories to fit the audience was what true storytellers always did.

The devils in the book are also based on devils that appear in southern tales. Because they assumed many different sizes and shapes in the stories I was told, I have felt free to put together a whole devil family in this book. Southern devils were always given human characteristics, and they tend to be appealing figures. Often it is easy to like these devils and to find them amusing. But it's important always to keep in mind that despite their lures they are still devils.

About the Author

William H. Hooks is the author of many books for middle readers, including *The 17 Gerbils of Class 4A, Crossing the Line,* and *The Mystery of Bleeker Street.* He has acted as educational consultant to the *Captain Kangaroo* show and ABC's Afterschool Specials. Currently he is the editor of *3 to Get Ready,* a children's magazine that appears as a Sunday supplement in newspapers across the country.

Mr. Hooks was born and raised in North Carolina and now lives in New York City.

About the Artist

Dirk Zimmer grew up in West Germany and attended the Academy of Fine Arts in Hamburg. He began illustrating for magazines and children's books after moving to the United States in 1977. His illustrations for *Felix in the Attic* by Larry Bograd received the Irma Simonton Black Award from Bank Street College of Education. Mr. Zimmer is currently at work on two science fiction books for children.